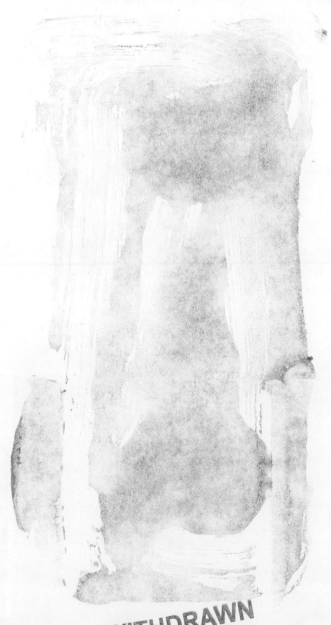

Benedict Finds a
Home

story and pictures by

Chris L. Demarest

Lothrop, Lee & Shepard Books / New York

Library of Congress Cataloging in Publication Data.
Demarest, Chris. Benedict finds a home. Summary:
Benedict leaves his crowded nest to search for the
perfect home. [1. Birds—Fiction. 2. Dwellings—
Fiction] I. Title. PZ7.D3914Be   [E]   81-15586
ISBN 0-688-00154-8   AACR2
ISBN 0-688-00586-1 (lib. bdg.)

*For Elizabeth
and Ashley*

Benedict lived in a crowded nest.

He had many brothers and sisters,
who were very noisy ...

and played with all of his toys.

One day he took off to find a nest of his own.

His first stop was the park.
"What luck," said Benedict, hurrying to settle in.

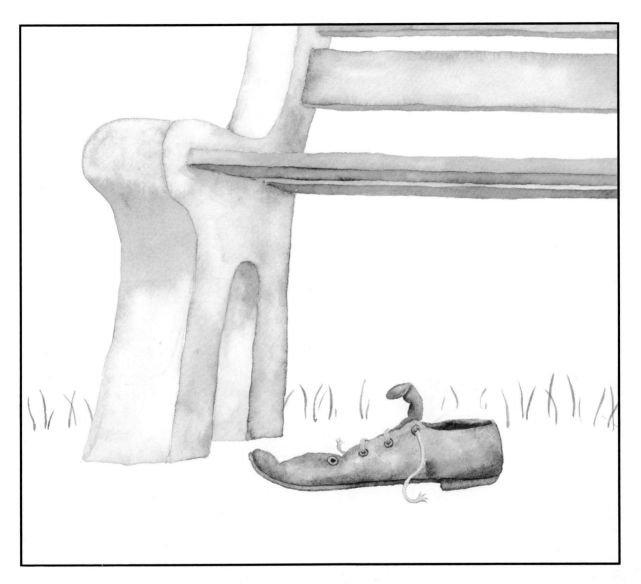

"A nest that's just right for one."

But it already belonged to someone else.

Next he spotted a shiny cave.
"Great," said Benedict.

"This looks clean and quiet."

But it wasn't quiet for long. BAROOM!

Poor Benedict. His ears were ringing.

Suddenly his face brightened.
Up ahead was the best place so far.

"Wow," said Benedict. "A nest with a view."

But the neighbors were not very friendly.

Benedict was having no luck.

Nothing was going right.

Just when he thought all was lost,
he spied the perfect home.

"Whew," said Benedict. "Safe at last."

But a sudden gust of wind sent him spinning.

Down he tumbled,

over and over,

until he landed ... THUMP!

"Ahhh," said Benedict. "Home ...

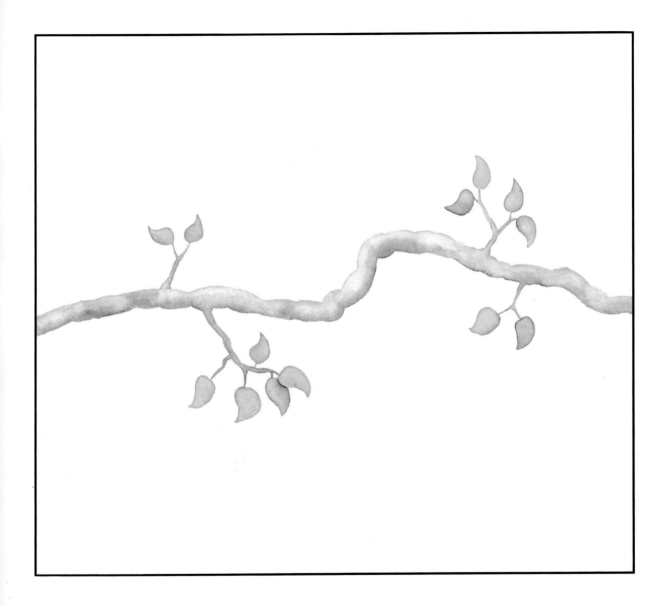

for now."